Best Bugs

by Becky Cheston
illustrated by Marsha Slomowitz

Harcourt
SCHOOL PUBLISHERS

Requests for permission to make copies of any part of the work should be addressed to School Permissions and Copyrights, Harcourt, Inc., 6277 Sea Harbor Drive, Orlando, Florida 32887–6777. Fax: 407-345-2418.

HARCOURT and the Harcourt Logo are trademarks of Harcourt, Inc., registered in the United States of America and/or other jurisdictions.

Printed in China

ISBN 13: 978-0-15-351676-4
ISBN 10: 0-15-351676-3

Ordering Options
ISBN 13: 978-0-15-351215-5 (Grade 5 Advanced Collection)
ISBN 10: 0-15-351215-6 (Grade 5 Advanced Collection)
ISBN 13: 978-0-15-358159-5 (package of 5)
ISBN 10: 0-15-358159-X (package of 5)

5 6 7 8 9 10   468   12 11 10 09

Pond Village usually came alive at about a quarter to dawn. This morning, as the sun's first pink rays burned through a light mist, Dapple the Dragonfly—*Dan* to his friends—was the first in his family to wake. Blinking his kaleidoscope eyes, he fluttered his wings, which were stiff from a long night's rest. Then he emerged from the overhang of sod and tree roots that he called home.

Dappled Dan was not the first in the village to rise. Perched on a reed that arched into the water, a familiar clique of girls chatted and preened. Glitter wafted her beautiful wings in and out, sending delicate rainbows shooting across the water. The twins, Polly and Chroma, copied Glitter's movements while Sheena flitted from one girl to the other, chattering. Now Ray appeared above Dan, zipping down in a zigzag pattern.

"Have you seen Hue yet?" Ray called out before he'd even set all of his six feet on the lily pad. "I'm starving."

"We could start our breakfast excursion without him, you know," Dan replied. "He'll know where to find us. Hey—did you see that evasive maneuver I managed yesterday?"

"That was awesome," Ray admitted. "There were two swallows on your tail when, all of a sudden—*zoop!*—you just dropped down and zigzagged out of there!"

"It was perfection, thank you very much." A gleeful Dan tipped one of his four gauzy wings in a salute and bowed. When he straightened, he spotted another dragonfly zipping toward him. It wasn't Hue, though—it was Sheena.

Sheena, never one to wait for an invitation, zoomed down to the lily pad. "You wouldn't happen to know where Hue is, would you?" she asked.

"No," said Dan. "Why?"

Sheena leaned in. "Glitter was just wondering," she said.

Ray rolled his eyes. The sun glinted off them and scattered in various directions. "Is she crazy?"

4

Sheena cocked her head to the side. "Maybe." Her laugh was suddenly cut off. "Hey—isn't that him now?" They all looked up. It was Hue all right—there was no mistaking that multicolored torso of emerald, purple, and midnight blue. "What a show-off!"

Hue was darting toward them at a dizzying pace, drawing a complex pattern of horizontal, vertical, and sloped lines. He hovered over the girls for a moment, then shot out and down until he was a mere inch from the water. Finally, he skimmed across the surface to the lily pad.

"'Morning, bugs!" Hue was giddy. He hopped onto the leaf. "Did you see those new maneuvers?" He noticed Sheena for the first time and tilted his wings at a flattering angle. "Are you coming to breakfast with us?"

It took less than five minutes for Dan to eat his fill: two mosquitoes, four gnats, and a tiny, winged water beetle that had strayed too far above the pond's surface. Sheena and Ray also found a quick, easy breakfast. Hue, meanwhile, was so busy darting, hovering, dropping, and zooming that he hadn't eaten a thing. Worse, he had attracted the first drowsy stragglers from the flock of swallows that nested near the pond.

Sheena was first to spot the birds. "Incoming!" she warned. Swiveling their eyes, they saw six or seven of the brown-and-white birds swoop swiftly down, up, and around the pond. However, the swallows were no match for the young dragonflies.

Dan zipped off back toward the lily pad, stopping to wait for the others in a clump of cattails. Ray and Sheena soon joined him. However, Hue continued to tease the swallows, hovering until one of the birds almost nabbed him, and then he darted off at top speed.

"Sort of a dangerous way to have fun," said Ray. "Ooh! That was really close!"

"I'll create a diversion while you two go get him," said Dan.

Soon after the three dragonflies jetted out from their cattail hideaway, Dan shot up toward a stand of willow trees, a position that put him in the flight path of three swallows. These birds were—unsuccessfully—in hot pursuit of Hue. Dan waited until the swallows were almost upon him before he dropped straight down then zoomed back up— a move he liked to call "The Zipper." Screeches of bird frustration echoed across the pond. Now Dan jetted off to the right. Swiveling one of his eyes in the opposite direction, he glimpsed Ray and Sheena dragging Hue back to the lily pad. Relieved, Dan turned again.

The shadow that fell over him came too late to act as a warning. Dan heard a loud *smack*. Pain bloomed between his eyes, and then everything went black.

Dan woke to the sight of two small, tawny eyes looking down at him from behind a slender beak. He tried to rise, but he could only move his head—painfully. "Don't eat me!" he pleaded, squinting his eyes shut. This was not how Dan had envisioned the end: immobilized and whining for mercy. He had thought it would be swifter. Why did he have so much time to think? Carefully, he opened one eye.

A young swallow hopped from one foot to the other, watching him with concern. Dan opened the other eye. Surprise rendered him speechless. A fat little spider moved back and forth, busily weaving. Something—besides the fact that he was pinned on his back—was wrong here. Through his muddled, sore head, it came to him.

Dan turned back to the swallow. "Why is she not lunch?" He motioned to the spider who had stopped spinning to join the bird.

"He's a vegetarian." It was the spider who answered.

"Which means..." Dan began.

"That's right," the swallow chirped. "I'm not going to eat *you,* either." The bird shuddered, as if revolted by the very thought. *"Yuck."*

"Then why am I here?"

"It's lucky you ran into Vinny," said the spider, "and I mean that quite literally."

"We sort of bumped into each other over the pond," said Vinny, hanging his head. "You passed out, and I flew you out of there quick. Otherwise . . . Well, let's just say I have a couple of aunts whose appetites are legend around these parts."

"Well . . . thanks, Vinny. I'm Dappled Dan." He tried to raise his head again and groaned.

"Careful, there," said the spider. "You've got a nasty bruise on the back of your head and a bent antenna. My name's Enid, by the way. Now, if you two don't mind, I'd like to finish my work."

2880927500

2880

sei2000

Vinny hopped a little closer. Dan flinched—a reflex. He'd never met a bird who didn't regard him as a tasty entrée. "Don't mind her," Vinny whispered. "She's sort of tired. I did drag her out of her web sort of early this morning."

"Why?"

"In order for her to fix you, of course," said Vinny.

"That's right," said Enid, her voice jiggling as she moved back and forth across one of Dan's wings. "You've got quite a tear here—and a rip on your top left wing, too. Good thing I know the dragonfly weave. When I'm done, you won't be able to tell they were even patched."

"What about this?" Dan pointed to the antenna that drooped into his face.

"I'll make a splint for you when I'm done over here," she said.

As Enid worked, Dan and Vinny talked. Vinny told him about his sisters who always made fun of his eating habits. One time, he explained, they'd snuck a mosquito into his berry/grass roll-up. Dan told Vinny about his friends, and how they passed the time at Pond Village. Vinny said he'd seen everyone—after all, bug-watching was the only way he could pass the time while the flock went hunting.

As they talked about Pond Village, Dan began to worry. "My friends and family," he said. "I bet they think I'm . . . well . . . gone."

"I'll get you back there," Vinny assured him. "However, you're in no condition to move now. Maybe tomorrow."

Tomorrow? By then everyone back home would have lost all hope—if they'd had any in the first place. Still, Dan supposed Vinny was right: There was nothing he could do about it now. Finally, relief at being among friends and exhaustion from his ordeal took its toll. When he closed his eyes so that Enid could splint his antenna, he felt himself dropping off to sleep.

When Dan woke, the sun was setting over the woods, spreading a weak amber light through the trees. Feeling was beginning to return to his sore wings, and there was a new ache in his throat. A feverish chill shook him to his core. Dan settled more deeply into his bed of leaves and fell back to sleep.

Hours later, he opened his eyes to find that a full moon illuminated everything in silver. Enid had been busy. Dan could see now that he was surrounded by a circle of small trees. Delicate webbing stretched from tree to tree, enclosing the area in a gauzy fence. He could see Enid resting in one of her cobwebs. Vinny slept nearby, his head tucked under one brown wing. An unlikely pair, his new friends were.

Dan missed his old friends, but he also felt a small ball of anger building in his thorax. Had they really given up on him so easily? His head aching, he dozed again. In his dreams, Dan flew around Pond Village, his feet wet from dipping into the water. He woke to find Vinny toweling him off with a leaf.

"Sorry, Dan," said Vinny. "I was trying to give you a drink of water."

Vinny refilled a hollowed-out acorn half and handed it over. Dan found he could sit up now, though his body shook as he drank. "Where's Enid?"

"Gathering some food. We figured you'd be hungry when you finally woke up."

Dan yawned. "How long have I been asleep?"

Vinny lifted a foot to count on his toes. "Three-and-a-half days."

"What?" Dan let out a heavy sigh. Apparently he had needed the rest. Still, it was as if he had ceased to exist. Had no one tried to find him? He felt certain that if Ray or Hue had disappeared, he would have combed these woods a thousand times over. Enid broke the gloom when she entered, carrying a silken sack full of precious treats—a mosquito, a beetle, and two tiny ants. As Dan ate, Vinny turned his back and hopped around the enclosure.

"*Eww!* Could you keep it down, please?" Vinny chirped. "I can hear you chew!"

After the meal and a quick wash, Vinny helped Dan to his wobbly feet so that he could walk around the enclosure. Then Enid inspected his wounds.

"You might be able to take that splint off tomorrow, but I wouldn't try flying for another couple of days."

"A couple more days?! I have to get back to Pond Village!" Dan protested.

"That's why," said the swallow, "you'll be traveling on Air Vinny."

Riding on top of a bird was nothing like flying on his own, Dan discovered. Vinny flew much higher than Dan usually did, so the air that streamed past him was cooler. He realized—after the panic of the first few minutes had subsided—that he could also see farther. The view was absolutely spectacular.

"We're getting closer!" Vinny yelled over the wind's roar. As Vinny began descending, Dan felt a splash of water smack him on the back.

"Hey!" Vinny turned his head to see a group of dragonflies zipping around. Among them were Hue and Ray. One of them hurled something at Vinny. The bird chirped in surprise and shook his head. A fragment of something pink fluttered to the ground.

"Water balloons!" Dan shouted. "We make them with rolled-up flower petals!"

"Not a good time for games!" cried Vinny, shaking off another one. The ride was suddenly becoming turbulent.

"They think I'm in trouble!" said Dan. "Hey—*guys!* It's okay! I don't need to be rescued!" Then Dan spotted something that made his heart drop into his stomach. In front of Vinny and Dan, two dragonflies hovered, holding a large net made from spider webbing. It was a trap—and they were going to fly into it full force. Dan imagined himself falling off Vinny's back and plunging to the ground. Some rescue! Dan closed his eyes. At that precise moment, Vinny tilted his beak and zoomed up just missing the trap.

Now that the trap had failed, Dan's friends circled around them, calling out: *Let him go! Kidnapper—release our friend! You'll never get away! Hey, Dan, are you all right?* Finally, one of them—Sheena—landed on Vinny's back and began whipping him with a blade of grass. When Dan got her to stop, he was able to explain what was going on.

Immediately, Sheena spread the word. Then the band of attackers became a dragonfly escort. For the rest of the ride, Dan relaxed into Vinny's feathers. Not only had his friends not forgotten him—they had plotted a daring rescue.

The trip was almost over. Some of the dragonflies had flown ahead to let Pond Village know Dan was safe and to help prepare for a welcoming feast. There would be special vegetarian items for Vinny, the guest of honor. Dan caught the first glimpse of the pond, a shiny silver coin in the sun. This had to be the highlight of his day. Then again, he thought, his friends' actions could be the pinnacle of this whole adventure . . . or meeting new friends, like Vinny and Enid . . . or flying on a bird . . . or dozing off to sleep on his way home.

Think Critically

1. Why doesn't Hue catch anything for breakfast?

2. When Hue engages in risky behavior, Dan sends Ray and Sheena to get him and then creates a diversion. What does this reveal about Dan's character?

3. List three details the author uses to show that Enid is skilled and hard-working.

4. What metaphor does the author use at the end of the book to describe the pond from a distance? Explain whether or not you think this description is effective.

5. What was your favorite part of this story? Why?

Social Studies

Map It! Brainstorm with family members to determine what parks, ponds, fields, swamps, or other natural ecosystems surround you. Make a map of your area including the places on your list. Ask family members to help you add to your map.

School-Home Connection Share this story with a family member. What are some other animal stories you and your family members enjoy?

Word Count: 2,268